BREAKFAST
AT THE
LIBERTY
DINER

Daniel Kirk

HYPERION BOOKS FOR CHILDREN

NEW YORK

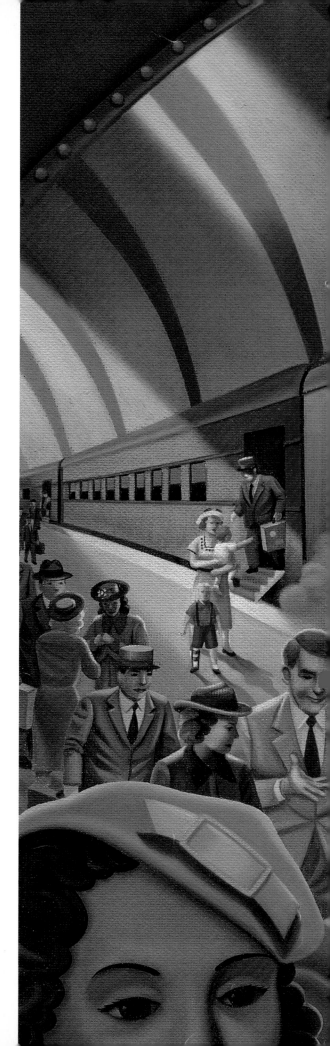

N ow arriving on track number one," a man's voice rattled over the loudspeakers, "the Twentieth Century Limited!" The doors of the train burst open and people spilled onto the platform. Bobby Potter eased himself down the steps, good leg first. Mrs. Potter squeezed out next with baby George struggling in her arms. The porter followed, swinging the heavy old suitcase and whistling a tune.

"Officer?" Mrs. Potter called, as they jostled their way through the crowd. "Can you tell me how to get to the Liberty Diner?"
"Sure thing, ma'am," the policeman smiled. "Just out of the station and left. You can't miss it!"
A pack of cameramen rushed past as a train screeched onto track number two.
Bobby shouted, "Uncle Angelo is going to meet us at the diner!"
"That's swell, kid," grinned the cop. "Maybe I'll see you there!"

At the diner, Bobby and his mother settled in at the counter. It was the first time since he'd been sick that Bobby had been away from home.

"Coffee, ma'am?" the counterman asked.

"Hey, Shorty!" a man shouted. "How about another cup of joe down here!"

"Hold your horses!" the counterman scowled. "Can't ya see I'm waitin' on the lady?"

"I'd like a cup of tea," Mrs. Potter said, "and a glass of milk for the baby. Bobby, for you?"

"Gimme a cup of joe," Bobby ordered.

His mother frowned. "He'll have a glass of milk, too."

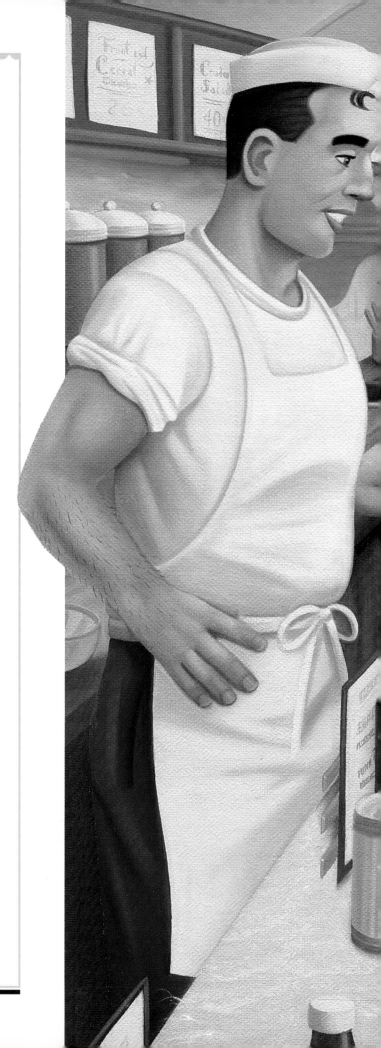

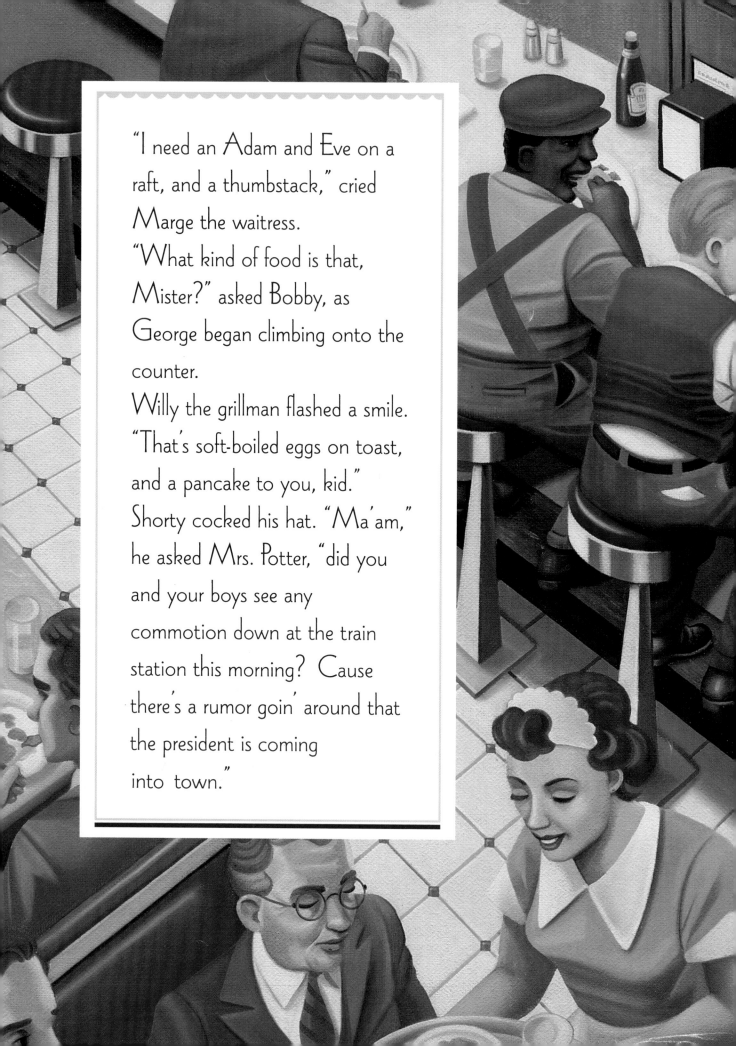

"I need an Adam and Eve on a raft, and a thumbstack," cried Marge the waitress.
"What kind of food is that, Mister?" asked Bobby, as George began climbing onto the counter.
Willy the grillman flashed a smile. "That's soft-boiled eggs on toast, and a pancake to you, kid."
Shorty cocked his hat. "Ma'am," he asked Mrs. Potter, "did you and your boys see any commotion down at the train station this morning? Cause there's a rumor goin' around that the president is coming into town."

"The president?" A man laughed. "It'll be a hot day in January when the president comes to THIS town."
Willy shook his head and flipped some hot cakes on the griddle. "I heard he's gonna talk to the factory men about their jobs."

"Oh, what a darling baby!" a lady cooed, as George noisily sucked his milk through a paper straw.

Bobby rolled his eyes. He reached into his pocket for the toy airplane his father had given him before he headed west, looking for work. It felt like he'd been gone a long time.

"A pair of cackles, wrecked!" cried Marge.

"*Wheeee!*" Bobby whistled through his teeth and waved his toy airplane overhead.

"Robert, put that away," his mother warned.

"I want some wrecked cackles, too," Bobby chimed in. "What are they?"

"Scrambled eggs, I think." His mother frowned. "Now put that toy away before you knock something over."

With the flick of a finger George toppled his glass onto its side. A sheet of milk spread across the counter, soaking napkins and newspapers.

"I'm so sorry," Mrs. Potter moaned, dabbing at the mess.

"He's always such a good baby!"

"Good at making a mess," Bobby mumbled.

The policeman from the train station charged into the diner. "Hey, Marge," he called, "clear two tables in the back, pronto! There's some important customers on their way."

"I don't like wrecked cackles," Bobby complained to his mother. "I can't eat them."

"They're your breakfast," she answered. "Eat them."

"I need a cluck and grunt and a stack of saddlebags!" cried Marge.

"Cute baby," said the policeman.

"Cute baby," Bobby grumbled.

The door flew open. Reporters from the train station burst in, followed by a handful of police and a half-dozen men in matching suits and hats. A round of flashbulbs exploded near the entrance.

George gleefully poured a mountain of salt onto the counter, as his mother craned her neck to see.

"Everybody get to your feet!" someone shouted.

"He's coming!"

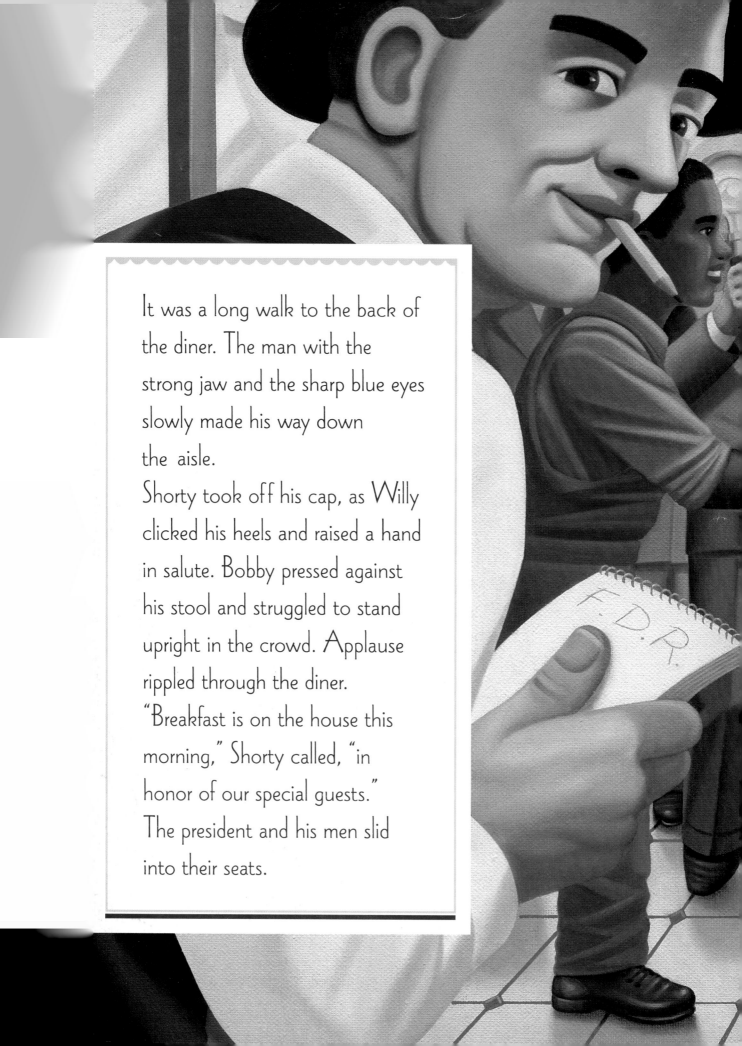

It was a long walk to the back of the diner. The man with the strong jaw and the sharp blue eyes slowly made his way down the aisle.

Shorty took off his cap, as Willy clicked his heels and raised a hand in salute. Bobby pressed against his stool and struggled to stand upright in the crowd. Applause rippled through the diner.

"Breakfast is on the house this morning," Shorty called, "in honor of our special guests." The president and his men slid into their seats.

Willy whispered to Marge, "When you serve him his eggs, could you get me an autograph?" Marge cuffed him on the shoulder. "You'd better make sure those eggs are cooked just right!"

"Say, lady," a reporter turned to Mrs. Potter. "It ain't every day you get to have breakfast with the president of the United States. How would you and the baby like to get a closer look?"

"Swell," Bobby scowled. "Maybe Georgie could throw some wrecked cackles on him."

"Robert!" Mrs. Potter cried. "Mind your manners!"

When the president had finished his breakfast, the Secret Servicemen moved swiftly to the door. A limousine waited outside. "Now's our chance!" the reporter said to Mrs. Potter. "Let me borrow your baby—I'm going to make him famous!"

The photographers raised their cameras as the reporter hoisted George through the crowd. "Mr. President!" he cried. "How about a special picture for the paper? You know the public loves babies."

The president steadied himself and took George in one arm. Then he saw Bobby swinging his leg against the stool. "Come on, young man." He smiled. "Let's get you in the picture, too."

Bobby held his toy airplane in a tight grip as the lights of the cameras flashed and stung his eyes.

"Nice plane," the president said. "Sometimes I fly in one that looks like that."

"My father gave it to me," said Bobby. "When I grow up I'm going to fly in an airplane, too!"

The president smiled. "Don't just fly *in* an airplane, son, *be the pilot.* Sail clear across the country and back again. Set your sights high. I know a boy like you can do anything he puts his mind to!"

Suddenly it was all over. George went crying back to his mother's arms, while the police, the reporters, the photographers, the president, and his men disappeared into the morning.

"He gets around pretty good for a guy with polio," a man said, his mouth full of toast.

"Hey, Sis!" Uncle Angelo called as he strode into the diner. "What's going on? The police had the roads all blocked off!"

"Angelo," Mrs. Potter cried,
"You'll never guess——"
Shorty waved and gave Bobby a
wink. "Next time you're in town,
kid, don't forget to bring the
president with you!"
Bobby waved back. "I won't
forget!"

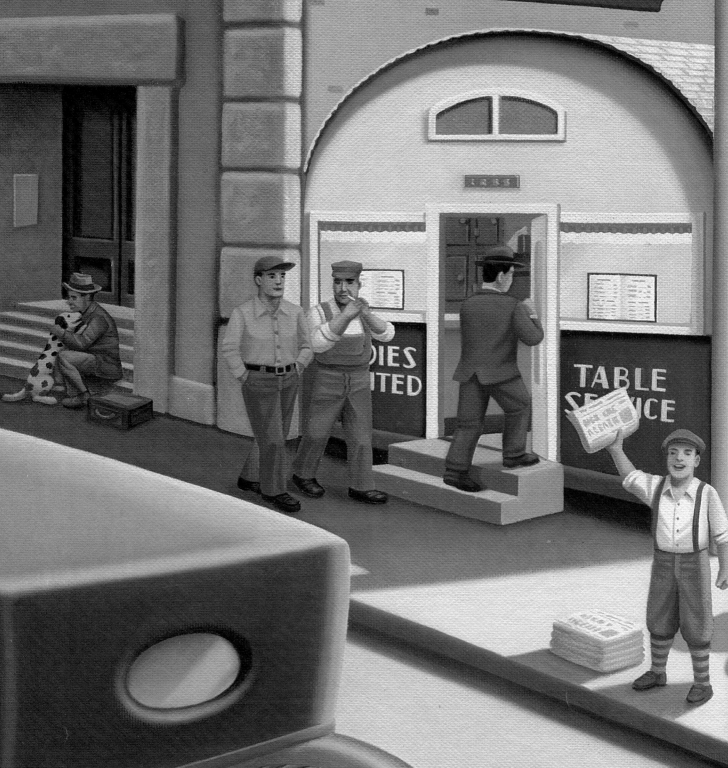

Bobby's picture with the president made the front page. Shorty had it framed and hung it by the door for all his customers to see.

In the spring, Mrs. Potter took her children to California, where her husband found a job. As the years passed and Bobby grew up and had children of his own, they always asked their daddy to get out the little toy airplane he had saved, and tell them about his breakfast at the Liberty Diner.

For my grandmother Margaret Collins Kirk,
who raised four sons during the depression years and later opened her diner,
Marge's Snack Shop, on Chicago's South Side.
—D. K.

Author's Note

There aren't many old-fashioned diners left on the roadways of America. Those that remain are a piece of our history, though to modern eyes they may look tired and worn. Once they were shiny and bright, with their barrel-vaulted ceilings, spinning chrome seats, and cozy booths. Diners in the 1930s served up cheap, simple home cooking, often 'round the clock. They were the kind of place where even a stranger could feel at home, settled in at the counter next to a couple of regulars, making small talk or skimming the headlines of the morning paper over a cup of joe. Customers got friendly, family-style service, and kids got to sit with grown-ups and feel like they were a part of the hurly-burly adult world.

Mostly mom-and-pop operations, diners were great places for kids to eat, even if they didn't give away a free toy with each meal. In the 1950s, I remember sitting at the counter with my brother and parents, watching the cook work his magic over the griddle, frying, tossing, whipping, scrambling, and slinging breakfast together before our very eyes.

In *Breakfast at the Liberty Diner*, Bobby Potter wears a brace on his leg to help him walk. Polio crippled millions of Americans during the first half of this century, including our thirty-second president, Franklin Delano Roosevelt. Despite physical hardships, Roosevelt served twelve years as president. He helped bring our country out of the Great Depression and steered the nation through some of the hardest years of World War II.

As a child, I was inspired by stories of Roosevelt and the example he set, and continue to be so today. In this book, I brought the president to Liberty Diner to give an ordinary American boy, Bobby, a message of inspiration and hope. This message is as true for a child today as it would have been to Bobby in the 1930s: Despite hardships and shortcomings, our future is what we make of it.

Research for the story and art took me in various directions. My wife and I often take our three children to a diner not far from home. Although a faded remnant of its early glory, the place still has charm—and good food! I also found *Diners*, by John Baeder, *American Diner*, by Richard Gutman, *FDR*, by Kenneth Davis, and *Roadside Magazine* helpful in documenting the style and period I was looking for. I owe a special debt of gratitude to Max's Diner in Harrison, New Jersey, and my models Raleigh, Russell, and Ivy Kirk, Julia and John Gorton, and Beth Trollan. ✦

Text and illustrations © 1997 by Daniel Kirk

For information address Hyperion Books for Children, 114 Fifth Avenue, New York, NY 10011-5690.

Printed in The United States of America.

First Edition

1 3 5 7 9 10 8 6 4 2

Library of Congress Cataloging-in-Publication Data
Kirk, Daniel.
Breakfast at the Liberty Diner / Daniel Kirk.
p.   cm.
Summary: Bobby, his mother, and his baby brother are having breakfast at the Liberty Diner when President Franklin Roosevelt stops in for a visit.
ISBN 0-7868-0303-7 (trade) — ISBN 0-7868-2243-0 (lib. bdg.)
[1. Diners (Restaurants) — Fiction. 2. Roosevelt, Franklin D. (Franklin Delano), 1882-1945—Fiction.] I. Title.
PZ7.K6339Br   1997
[E]—dc20   96-31989

This book is set in 22-pt Wade Sans Light Plain.

Designed by Julia Gorton
The artwork for each picture is prepared using oil paint on canvas.